How King Montezuma Got His Revenge

Annalisa Nash Fernandez

illustrated by

Pilar Castillo Layos

Ethnic Ethos Books

Ethnic Ethos Books
POB 141453
Coral Gables, FL 33134
EthnicEthosBooks@gmail.com

Printed in the United States of America
First Printing, 2016
First edition

Copyright © 2016 Annalisa Nash Fernandez

All rights reserved. This book or any portion thereof
may not be reproduced or used in any manner whatsoever
without the express written permission of the publisher
except for the use of brief quotations.

Published by Createspace
North Charleston, SC

ISBN-13: 978-1535553476
ISBN-10: 1535553472
Library of Congress Control Number: 2016918331

History is made by leaders

who invent, inspire, or just plain rule.
But sometimes there is more to the story
than what you learn in school.
By the legend of King Montezuma,
you can go to Mexico for a great time,
but a stinky curse from Aztec history
will hit you from behind . . .

Five centuries ago,

millions of people in the Mexican Valley formed the Aztec Empire, an educated and prosperous society. Their capital was as large as Paris and other great cities of Europe, and their stone temples and pyramids outnumbered those in Egypt.

The Aztecs ruled far and wide,

but to the Spaniards they lost it all,

and as travelers' legends have it,

Montezuma seeks revenge for that fall.

For it was he who opened the stone gates

to those from a faraway land,

so when people come to Mexico today,

Montezuma ensures he has the upper hand.

Aztec civilization once was on top

because they valued education.

Kids studied architecture and astrology,

learning math and time on stone creations.

You could say school attendance

is an Aztec thing,

as the first society to educate not just the rich,

but every human being.

Farming paid the Aztecs' bills –

through invention they grew with ease.
Floating gardens stayed watered
to grow squash, beans, and spicy chilies.
Corn was ground by stone for tortillas,
and popped to decorate their headdress,
while for money they used coffee beans,
which for trading were most precious.

Cocoa beans and chili peppers

made a beverage that was special.

Saved for warriors and ceremonies,

Montezuma drank it on a regular schedule.

It tasted bitter and spicy —

nothing like the sweet cocoa you drink up.

That took international teamwork

with sugar brought from Europe.

Aztecs enjoyed many activities,

like music, art, sports, and religion,

but it's also well known that sacrifice

was a big part of Aztec tradition.

Priests played music through shells,

burning tree sap as incense,

and cast doves into the stream

for Gods to send rain and presents.

"Flower Wars" were for training

and chance to show off military skills.

Regular wars used darts and stones,

but these were expert weapon drills.

The battle sacrifice was a gift to the Gods

to keep the sun moving from heaven.

So Aztecs were well trained to fight enemies,

but not very good at recognizing them . . .

Hernán Cortés arrived on horseback,

armed with fancy Spanish weaponry

to conquer the Aztec capital of *Tenochtitlan,*

now known as Mexico City.

Horses were new to the Americas,

on the Spaniards' ships they went.

The Aztecs saw a man with horse legs,

and thought he was Godsent.

The *Conquistadores* were in awe

of Aztec kinship and civilization.

Cortés sent letters back to Spain

describing the Aztecs with admiration.

Montezuma welcomed Cortés as a God,

ordering his warriors not to attack.

But the Spanish army took the King prisoner,

and then the forces couldn't be held back.

The Aztecs had the advantage

of being numerous and wise.

But the Spaniards carried

a deadly weapon in disguise.

Disease brought from Europe

sealed the Aztec Empire's fate:

the mighty civilization destroyed

because Montezuma opened the gate.

In Mexico today,

the mighty Aztecs are long gone.

But in this modern legend,

Montezuma's spirit lives on.

You foreigners are still welcome

to vacation on Mexican land,

but when the airplane gates open,

Montezuma will take command.

Dancing the "Aztec two-step,"

asking "*¿dónde está el baño por favor?,*"

you're under attack from Montezuma

as you run to the bathroom door.

Your tummy extends and rumbles,

and the *tacos* in it spin.

Then you realize this is a battle

that your butt won't win.

The forces can't be held back,

and there is a thunderous blast

of *nachos* and *enchiladas verdes*,

powered by stinky gas.

Tourists plead *ayúdame*

for this modern day battle to end.

And that's how King Montezuma

finally got his revenge.

Acknowledgments

Historical artwork featured is in the public domain in its country of origin and in other countries and areas where the copyright term is the author's life plus 100 years or less, including works by Diego Rivera, the Conquest of Mexico series, the Codex Magliabechiano, and the Codex Mendoza, and Antonio de Leon y Gama.

Cover art: The Conquest of Tenochtitlan, from the Conquest of Mexico series, representing the 1521 Fall of Tenochtitlan.

Original artwork is authorized for commercial use by the author.

Disclaimer

"Foreign" is a relative concept, and the real culprit for intestinal distress while travelling is not Montezuma but enterotoxigenic bacteria foreign to the host that thrive worldwide under the pseudonyms Delhi Belly, Rangoon Runs, Mummy's Tummy, Bali Belly, Teheran Tummy, Thai-del Wave, Tokyo Trots, Poonah Pooh, Hong Kong Dog, Casablanca Crud, Greek Gallop, Rome Runs, Singapore Shakes et al.; not only "Montezuma's Revenge."

About the Author

Annalisa Nash Fernandez lives in Connecticut with her husband and three children, one of which was born while living in Mexico City. Maybe he's why she was spared from Montezuma's Revenge.

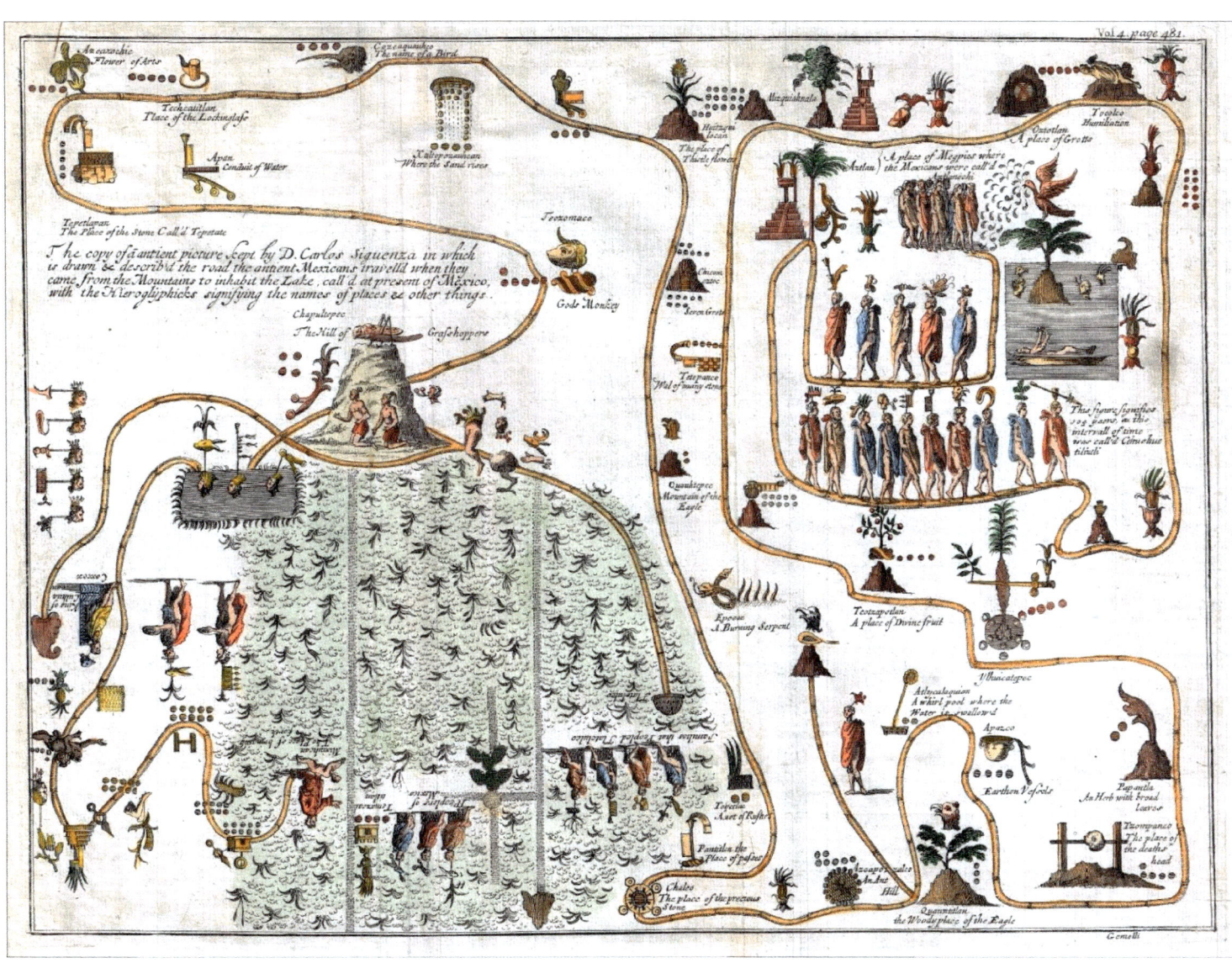

Gemelli Careri's map of the Aztec migration from Aztlan to Chapultapec from *Voyage Round the World*, 1704

Manufactured by Amazon.ca
Bolton, ON